Just Like That

PRAISE FOR *STORYSHARES*

"One of the brightest innovators and game-changers in the education industry."
– Forbes

"Your success in applying research-validated practices to promote literacy serves as a valuable model for other organizations seeking to create evidence-based literacy programs."

- Library of Congress

"We need powerful social and educational innovation, and Storyshares is breaking new ground. The organization addresses critical problems facing our students and teachers. I am excited about the strategies it brings to the collective work of making sure every student has an equal chance in life."
– Teach For America

"Around the world, this is one of the up-and-coming trailblazers changing the landscape of literacy and education."
- International Literacy Association

"It's the perfect idea. There's really nothing like this. I mean wow, this will be a wonderful experience for young people."   - Andrea Davis Pinkney, Executive Director, Scholastic

"Reading for meaning opens opportunities for a lifetime of learning. Providing emerging readers with engaging texts that are designed to offer both challenges and support for each individual will improve their lives for years to come. Storyshares is a wonderful start."
- David Rose, Co-founder of CAST & UDL

Just Like That

Jannette LaRoche

STORYSHARES

Story Share, Inc.
New York. Boston. Philadelphia

Storyshares
Story Share, Inc.
24 N. Bryn Mawr Avenue #340
Bryn Mawr, PA 19010-3304
www.storyshares.org

Inspiring reading with a new kind of book.

Interest Level: High School
Grade Level Equivalent: 2.3

9781642611618

Book design by Storyshares

Printed in the United States of America

Storyshares Presents

1

"You just ran a red light."

Tom looked over at Meera and smiled. "I know," Tom said. "It's called dodging. Everyone is doing it. It's fun.

"Seems dangerous," Meera replied.

"That's the point," Tom said.

Meera went back to looking at her phone.

Tom felt angry. He'd borrowed his neighbor's car to impress Meera. His dad let him drive all the time, even though he was only fifteen. But his dad wasn't home and Tom really wanted Meera to like him.

"Watch this." Tom pressed hard on the gas. The car flew past the stop sign. Meera never looked up. He thought he should try something else.

"I bet you didn't know you were with a celebrity," Tom said.

"What? Who?"

Tom smiled. "Me. Tom Cruz. Get it? Like the actor?"

"That's funny." Meera's laugh sounded mean.

Tom had had enough. Meera was one of the prettiest girls in school, but she wasn't nice. His best friend, Evan, had said so. Tom just didn't want to believe it. All he could think about was getting the chance to kiss her.

Tom was so upset that he ran through another red light. This time it wasn't on purpose. He didn't notice it until he was halfway across the street. Then all he could see was the front of another car coming right at him. At the last second, it turned to the side with a screech of tires.

"Holy crap! Did you see that?"

"What now?" Meera hadn't looked up once from the text she was sending.

With his heart beating hard, Tom was more careful the rest of the way home. He pulled into his neighbor's driveway and left the keys in the glove box. It didn't look like Mr. Smith had noticed the car was even gone.

Meera finally put away her phone and looked at Tom.

"That was fun," she said. "Want to walk me home?"

Tom couldn't believe it. Half of him wanted to tell her off. The other half still hoped to get a chance to kiss her.

"Hey, Tom!" It was Evan. He lived four houses down. "Want to play some video games?"

"Maybe later. I'm taking Meera home."

He hoped Evan would get the hint. Evan didn't.

"I can drive her home," Evan said. He'd turned sixteen a month ago. He loved to rub it in Tom's face whenever he could.

"Thanks," Meera said. "It's not too far."

Tom had to ride in the back. It was full of fast food wrappers and empty soda cans. Worst of all, it smelled like rotten milk.

At Meera's house, Tom jumped out and opened the door for her.

"Thanks for the ride." She smiled at Evan and Tom felt jealous. Meera should like him, not Evan. All Evan did was give her a ride home. Tom had stolen a car and almost gotten killed.

"I guess I'll see you tomorrow," Tom said.

"You could come in for a while," Meera told him.

"Maybe next time," Tom said. He was too mad. He didn't even want to kiss her anymore. He got back in the car and slammed the door.

"Why did you turn her down?" Evan asked. "I thought you liked her."

"She's boring."

"What did you guys do?" Evan asked as he drove Tom home.

Tom told Evan about Mr. Smith's car. He told him Meera didn't even pay attention while he was dodging. Evan's older brother Chris had taken them dodging their first time last year.

"I told you so," Evan smiled.

"Yeah, you did," Tom agreed.

"You could have borrowed my car."

"Your car stinks," Tom said. "And I thought Meera would think I was bad if I stole a car."

"Mr. Smith lets people borrow it all the time," Evan said.

"Yeah, but she doesn't know that."

Evan laughed. His laugh was real and made Tom feel better.

"Did you at least have fun?" Evan asked.

"At first. Then I almost got in an accident."

"For real?"

Tom blushed. "I ran a red light."

"That's the point of dodging," Evan said.

"But it was an accident," Tom said. "I was mad at Meera and didn't check to see if anyone was coming."

"I guess I'm glad you didn't take my car."

2

They played video games until Evan's mom said it was time for dinner. Then Tom went home and waited for his little brother, Joey. Joey went to daycare until six o' clock. Most nights his mom picked him up in between her two jobs.

Tom cooked macaroni and cheese and set the table. His mom and Joey got home at seven o' clock. The food was cold and Tom was starving.

"I thought I told you I'd be late," Tom's mom said.

She took off the vest she wore at the grocery store and threw it in the corner. She hated that job. Her real job was as a nurse's aide at a nursing home. She worked nights so she could be home with them after school. But his dad had gotten hurt at work two years ago and couldn't do his job. They needed the extra money.

"Where's your dad?" Tom's mom asked.

"I don't know," Tom said. "He wasn't here when I got home."

His mom looked like she wanted to cry or hit someone. Sometimes his dad left for days at a time. When he got home, he always said he was sorry. His mom would yell and they would fight. Then they would make up and it would be okay for a while.

Tom's mom shook her head. Lately she was too tired to fight. "Thanks for making dinner," she said. "It looks great."

Tom heated the food up in the microwave. After they ate, he helped Joey with his homework while their mom took a nap.

Joey was a real smart kid. He was ten, but sometimes he helped Tom with *his* homework. It wasn't that Tom was stupid. He just didn't like school.

* * *

That night, Tom dreamed about the car that almost hit him. In his dream, it didn't turn. It ran right into Mr. Smith's car. Tom woke up sweating. He had been very lucky no one had gotten hurt. He promised himself he would never do anything that stupid again.

3

"Did you hear about Jenna Thompson?"

Tom heard that question all over school the next day. The answer was always different. Some people said a bus hit her. Some people said it was a car. Some people said she jumped in front of a train. She was dead or alive or in a coma or perfectly fine. It all depended on who you asked.

Tom remembered Jenna from grade school. They had gone to daycare together even though they went to different schools at the time. She was very quiet, and some of the other kids picked on her. Tom had thought she was nice, and they became friends. He'd made sure no one bothered her.

Tom stopped going to daycare in middle school. He didn't see Jenna again until they started high school. She had changed a lot by then. She had friends, was in the band, and took all the hard classes. Tom was in the easy classes, but they had gym together. She didn't seem to remember him at all.

Then one day, they ran into each other in the hall. He was hurrying to get to class, late as usual. He ran around the corner and smacked right into Jenna. Her books went all over and he helped her pick them up.

"Thanks, Tom," she said when he was done.

"You remember me?" Tom asked.

"Of course," Jenna said. This made Tom feel warm inside. "I remember you, but..." Tom knew he wouldn't like what she said next. "I guess we're pretty different now."

"Yeah. I guess so," Tom said.

Tom handed her the last book and walked away. He didn't even say goodbye. That was the last time they talked. He knew she was too smart and pretty for someone like him. But he'd also thought she was too nice to care.

Now he felt bad for never taking the time to apologize. He would feel awful if that was the last conversation they ever had.

* * *

Evan caught up to Tom after fourth hour.

"Did you hear about that girl?" Evan asked.

Tom nodded. Evan didn't know he and Jenna used to be friends. Evan had moved in down the street in seventh grade. By then, Tom was already staying home alone after school. He never told Evan about the talk he and Jenna had.

"I heard if she dies, we'll get a day off school," Evan said.

Tom looked at Evan like he was speaking a different language. "That's disgusting," Tom said.

Evan shrugged. "It's not like we know her."

"I have to get to class," Tom said.

He saw the confused look on Evan's face. They had never argued before. Tom just didn't think Evan could understand. Even though he wasn't friends with Jenna anymore, he still cared about her.

At lunch, Tom saw Jenna's best friend, Sandy. She was sitting at a table with a plate of food in front of her. She hadn't taken a single bite. Several girls hugged her or patted her arm as she cried. He wanted to ask her what the real story was, but there were too many people around.

It turned out he didn't need to.

Ten minutes before the last class ended, the principal made an announcement. "Attention students. As you may know, Jenna Thompson was hit by a car yesterday afternoon. She was badly injured, but her parents report she is in stable condition now. If anyone would like to talk to a counselor about this, they will be available after school. Thank you."

Tom let out a huge sigh of relief. Jenna would be okay. As soon as she got back to school, he would talk to her.

He remembered his dream from the night before. It was weird that he dreamed about getting hit by a car and Jenna really did.

All of a sudden, Tom felt sick. He had a terrible feeling. When the bell rang, he took a long time getting up. If he missed the bus he would have to walk home. He had to check on something, though.

In the school's library, he waited for a computer to open up. They were only supposed to be used for homework. Most people checked email and looked up other stuff when the librarian wasn't looking. Tom hardly ever came here unless he had to for class.

Finally, he got on the computer and did a search. After a few tries, he found the newspaper article about Jenna's accident. He read it three times, but the words didn't change. The car that hit Jenna had swerved when another car ran a red light.

And he had been driving that other car.

4

Tom was surprised to see his father's car when he got home.

"Hey, buddy. How was school?"

His dad was on the couch drinking an energy drink. Tom didn't know what he needed energy for. All he did was watch TV when he was home.

"You didn't come home last night," Tom said.

Tom didn't usually talk back to his dad. He was a big man, over a foot taller than Tom. He never hit his kids. He didn't have to. All he had to do was flex his muscles and they were too afraid to do anything wrong.

Today, Tom had scarier things to worry about than his dad.

"Sorry about that," his dad said. "I was out with my buddies and lost track of time."

"I'll remember that the next time I come home late," Tom said.

"Are you backtalking me, boy?" Tom's dad asked.

"Mom was worried about you," Tom said.

His mom had stopped worrying about his dad years before. But his dad didn't need to know that.

"I said I was sorry. I'll make it up to her. And you boys, too. How about we go fishing this weekend?"

"Sure. Sounds great," Tom said.

"All right. You get your homework done."

Tom knew his dad didn't really care if he did his homework or not. He just wanted to get rid of him. That was fine with Tom. He needed to be alone.

In his room, Tom reread the article he had printed out. It said an old man driving with his wife swerved to miss a car running a red light. When he turned, he hit Jenna, who was standing on the sidewalk. The police did not give the older man driving that car a ticket. They wanted to find the driver of the car that ran the red light.

Tom didn't know what to do. The police only knew that the car that ran the red light was red. The couple in the car that hit Jenna didn't get a good look at it. No one else saw what happened except Jenna. The paper said she had a brain injury and was in a coma. She could be fine, or she might never wake up. Or she could die.

What Tom needed was more information.

* * *

His dad cooked dinner that night. Tom guessed he must still feel guilty about not coming home the night before. Grilled chicken and mashed potatoes were a lot better than anything Tom could make. They went a long way in helping him forgive his dad.

Tom's mother must have felt the same way. The fight they usually had after he went away never happened.

"How was school today?" Tom's mom asked.

Joey told everyone about the dinosaur his class was making. He was so excited, he talked through the whole dinner. Tom was glad no one asked him about his day. When everyone was done eating, he offered to wash the dishes.

"You were pretty quiet tonight," Tom's mom said as she started drying them.

"I can do that, Mom," Tom said. "You should go rest."

"I had a short shift at the store today so I got a good nap in this morning. And I think you're changing the subject."

"I'm just tired, I guess," Tom said.

"I heard about the accident yesterday. Wasn't that the girl you used to be friends with when you were little?" Tom's mom asked.

Tom felt like his blood had turned to ice. Why was his mother asking about Jenna? Did she know something?

"I think so," Tom said. He chose his words carefully. "We aren't really friends anymore."

"What a tragedy," Tom's mom said. "It scares me to death to think it could have been one of my boys."

Tom began to relax. She was just being a mother.

"I hope they catch that other driver," she said.

Tom's good feelings disappeared. He really wanted to ask his mom if the whole thing was the other driver's fault. But he was afraid she would figure out it was him. She had too much else to worry about.

"What is it, honey? "Tom's mom asked.

"Nothing," Tom said. "I just hope she gets better."

His mom finished drying and kissed the top of his head. She had to stand on her tiptoes to reach. He usually hated that, but it felt nice to know she cared. Would she still love him if she knew the truth?

Just Like That

5

Three days later, Tom finally got a chance to talk to Sandy. She was at her locker by herself after school. It was the first time he had seen her alone since the accident. He knew if he didn't talk to her right away he would lose his nerve.

"Hey, Sandy," Tom said.

"What do you want?" She sounded angry.

"I'm Tom Cruz. I used to be friends with Jenna."

"So?" Sandy asked.

"Well, I just wondered how she was doing."

"She got hit by a car. How do you think she's doing?"

Tom made fists with his hands to control his temper. "Is she awake yet?" he asked.

"Why do you care?" Sandy asked. "You know, I'm sick of people thinking what happened is exciting. My best friend almost died."

"She was my friend once, too," Tom replied.

"Well, not anymore. She doesn't need trash like you in her life," Sandy said.

Tom felt like punching the wall. Or maybe Sandy.

"I'm not trash," he said. He wanted to sound calm and mad, but it sounded more like he was about to cry.

"Whatever," Sandy said. "Just stay away from Jenna. Haven't you hurt her enough?"

Sandy slammed her locker and walked away.

Tom stood for a long time thinking about what she said. Did Sandy know he had been driving the other car? Is that what she meant about hurting Jenna? Or had he done something else?

He remembered the one time they'd talked last year. He had been mad at Jenna for saying that they were so different. But he was the one who had walked away. Maybe he had hurt her feelings too.

This only made Tom feel worse. Plus, he had missed his bus again. The long walk home gave him lots of time to think.

He knew he had made a mistake by taking Mr. Smith's car and running the red light. He never meant for anyone to get hurt. If telling the truth would help Jenna get better, he would do it. But he would also get in trouble. Tom wished someone could tell him what to do.

When he got home, he found Evan playing basketball in his driveway.

"Did you miss the bus again?" Evan asked.

"Yeah." Tom dropped his backpack and took the ball from Evan.

"I could have given you a ride," Evan said. "All you have to do is ask."

"I didn't know I was going to miss the bus, did I?" Tom didn't mean to yell at Evan, but he was so upset he couldn't help it.

"Whoa. Sorry I asked. What's wrong with you, anyway?"

"Just had a bad day," Tom said. "I didn't mean to snap at you."

Tom tossed the ball to Evan. They shot baskets in silence for a few minutes. Tom tried to think of a way to talk to Evan about the accident.

"Have you heard anything more about that girl that got hit by the car?" Tom asked.

"Only that she's doing about the same," Evan said.

"Where did you hear that?" Tom wanted to know.

"My mom works at that hospital, remember?" Evan said. "Word gets around. She's still in her coma. She broke some bones, but they say her brain is going to be okay. They think she'll wake up soon."

"That's good." Tom was very relieved.

"It's weird, isn't it? That someone can just be walking down the street and almost die? Seems like it's safer to be driving than walking," Evan said.

Tom waited to see if Evan would say anything else. He thought Evan might remember Tom had been out driving the same time Jenna got hit. But Evan didn't say anything else about it. After a while, they decided to go play video games.

6

When Tom got home, he looked to see if his dad had the day's newspaper. Sometimes he bought one to look for jobs. He got paid a small amount from getting hurt at work, but it wasn't much. Most times he didn't mind, but sometimes he felt bad about Tom's mom having to work two jobs.

Tom found a newspaper and looked through it for information about the accident. He felt like it should be front-page news. But the only article he saw was on page fourteen. He read it a dozen times.

The police still had no idea who was driving the car that ran the red light. It said the driver had only committed a misdemeanor. They urged the driver to come forward and were still looking for anyone who saw it happen.

Tom felt relieved. The police had no idea it was him. They didn't even know it was Mr. Smith's car. He thought about what the article said. All he had done wrong was run a red light.

They said it was only a misdemeanor.

A small charge.

He probably wouldn't even get a ticket for something like that.

Except he didn't have a driver's license. And Jenna had almost died.

Hundreds of people ran red lights all the time. Was it really his fault that things turned out the way they did?

Tom thought back to what Sandy had said about him. She said he was trash. He knew his parents didn't make as much money as other people. He wasn't as good in school as people like Jenna and Sandy. He didn't think that meant he wasn't as good as anyone else, though.

If he told everyone what he did, they would all think he was a criminal. Why should he tell the truth when people already said bad things about him? Tom decided then and there that he would never say another word about the accident.

What was done was done, and nothing good would come from telling the truth.

Just Like That

7

Tom felt much better after he made up his mind not to say anything about the accident. He wanted his life to go back to being normal.

After school on Friday, he went to Evan's house to play video games. He knew Evan's mom might have heard something about Jenna, but he didn't ask.

"Want to go out to the movies tomorrow?" Evan asked.

"Sounds good," Tom said.

"The thing is, I wanted to ask Allison out."

Evan had been in love with Allison Combs since sixth grade.

"So why are you asking me?"

"I thought she would be more likely to say yes if it was a double date." Evan winked at Tom. "And I thought that would be a good excuse for you to ask Meera out again."

Tom felt sick for a moment. The last time he had taken Meera out had been a disaster. Tom didn't think he could go out with Meera again. He was sure he wouldn't be able to enjoy himself at all. But Evan didn't know about the accident. He had to think of something else to say.

"I thought you didn't like Meera," Tom said. "Besides, I don't think she likes me.

"Don't be crazy. She wanted you to stay at her house after I took her home. I'm telling you, she likes you. You're just too chicken to go for it."

"I am not," Tom said.

Evan smiled. Tom realized he couldn't back out now. He would have to ask Meera out or Evan would make fun of him. And really, he did like Meera. Maybe if he was with Evan and Allison it wouldn't be so bad.

"Fine. I'll call her," Tom said.

Evan handed Tom his phone.

"Now?" Tom asked.

"Yeah. I have to know if she says yes before I can call Allison."

Tom found Meera's phone number in his backpack and punched in the numbers. She picked up on the second ring.

"Hey, Meera. It's Tom Cruz."

"Like the actor?" she laughed.

Tom was glad she remembered.

"That's the one. What's up?" Tom said.

"Not much," replied Meera.

Evan made kissing expressions and Tom stuck out his tongue. He had to take the phone in the next room before he could ask the next question.

"I was wondering if you want to go to the movies tomorrow night," Tom said. "Evan can drive us."

"Sounds like fun."

"Really?" Tom couldn't believe how easy that was.

"Yeah," Meera said. "What time will you guys pick me up?

Tom covered the phone and asked Evan, but he only shrugged his shoulders.

"Can I call you tomorrow?" Tom asked. "We don't know which movie yet."

"Sure. I'll talk to you then," Meera said.

She hung up and Tom stood looking at the phone. He felt really good. All week he had worried about the accident and Jenna. Maybe the best thing to do was get back to real life.

He gave the phone back to Evan, who called Allison. Before long, their double date was all planned.

The rest of the weekend was great. Tom didn't really enjoy the chick flick Meera and Allison wanted to see, but at least he got to hold Meera's hand. And when Evan dropped Meera off at home, Tom walked her to the door and kissed her.

Meera smiled at him. "We should go out again sometime," she said.

"Yeah. I'd like that," Tom replied.

Just Like That

8

On Sunday, Tom woke up happy for the first time in a week. He hadn't had any bad dreams. He wasn't worried about anyone finding out about the accident. Life seemed like it was back to normal.

He felt so good he even took Joey to the park to play basketball. They didn't get to spend much time together. Usually, the only time they hung out was while they were doing homework.

Joey seemed very happy to be with Tom. That made Tom feel even better.

Tom's mom didn't have to work either job that day. After she took her nap, she made a great dinner. She was the best cook in the house. Tom's dad was even home and they felt like a real family. It didn't happen very often. Tom took that as a sign he had made the right decision not to say anything about the accident.

* * *

After dessert, everyone sat down to watch TV together. Sunday evening cartoons used to be Tom's favorite, but he didn't get to watch them much anymore. Joey made a fuss when his mom said he had to go to bed. Tom was glad he was old enough to stay up later.

Tom's dad didn't tell him to go to bed when the news came on, so Tom stayed to watch. He didn't really care much about the news, but he liked being able to stay up with his dad.

They watched a story about a war somewhere, then the weather. Tom was about to call it a night when he heard what the next story would be.

The case of the girl who was hit by a car earlier this week takes a turn. Stay tuned for more information.

Tom was nervous all through the commercials. Had something worse happened to Jenna? Had the police figured out something about the other car? Finally, the reporter came back on.

Tom held his breath as he listened to the story. The good news was that Jenna was awake. It looked like she was going to be just fine. Her parents were on the TV saying she would make a full recovery. Tom almost laughed out loud with relief.

Then he heard the bad news.

The man driving the car that hit her, Mr. Applewood, had a heart attack that morning. His wife came on to say that he was very upset about what had happened. She said her husband felt like he should have done something different. He felt so guilty about the accident that his heart had given out on him. He was alive, but would have to have surgery.

Tom felt like he couldn't breathe. He had thought it wouldn't help anyone for him to tell the truth. But if he had, maybe Mr. Applewood wouldn't have had a heart attack.

Now, Tom was more confused than ever.

9

Tom stood at the end of the hallway for a long time. He had snuck out of school before lunch to come to the hospital. Now that he was here, he didn't know if he could do what he'd planned.

All week, he'd worried about what to do. He tried to act like nothing was wrong, but it didn't work. He should have been having a great time. He and Meera had another date planned for the next day. His mom and dad hadn't fought in almost two weeks. But all he could think about was the accident.

His first concern was Mr. Applewood. When Tom had run the red light, it had been an accident. He wouldn't have done it if he had seen the other car coming. At the time, he had no way of knowing Jenna had been hit.

But he had chosen to keep quiet about it. Then Mr. Applewood had a heart attack from feeling so guilty. That was one hundred percent Tom's fault.

Tom was also afraid of what might happen with Jenna. He had read in the paper that Mr. and Mrs. Applewood barely saw the car Tom was driving. They only knew it was red. But Jenna might have seen it better before she got hit. Now that she was awake, would she tell the police?

Tom felt like he had to do something or he would go crazy.

He couldn't do anything about Mr. Applewood. Tom couldn't tell the old guy it wasn't his fault. Not without admitting he had been driving the other car. Since he'd never met Mr. Applewood before, he had no reason to even talk to him.

Jenna was a different story. They had been friends once. If Tom could talk to her, he could find out if she had seen the car. And maybe he would feel better.

Tom found out from Evan that Jenna was doing a lot better. She could have visitors now. Tom was afraid to go to the hospital after school when her friends would be there. So he decided to leave school early on Friday. He would probably get in trouble for skipping class, but it was worth it.

Now that he was here, he didn't know what to say. Jenna might not want to talk to him. After all, Sandy thought he was trash. Maybe Jenna did, too. Or maybe she wouldn't even remember him.

"Are you lost, honey?" a nurse in a blue top with teddy bears asked him.

"No. I'm here to see a friend," Tom said.

The nurse smiled. "Do you know what room he's in?"

"Yeah. She's in room 303," Tom said.

"Oh, you mean Jenna?" asked the nurse.

Tom nodded, and the nurse put her hand on his shoulder. "Are you afraid to see her?" she asked.

"How did you know?" Tom asked.

"When someone has been badly hurt, it hurts the people who care about them, too. It can be scary to see a friend in pain. But Jenna is doing great. I'm sure she'd love to have a friend to talk to."

"Thanks," Tom said.

He was still scared, but he couldn't tell the nurse why. But now she was watching him, so he had to go in.

Jenna didn't look as bad as he had feared. Her leg was in a cast and her arm was in a sling. She had some bruises on her face. Part of her head had been shaved. He thought it made her look kind of tough. Her eyes were closed, but she opened them when he stood by her bed.

10

"Tom?"

"Hey, Jenna. I heard what happened. I hope you don't mind me visiting."

"Of course not," Jenna said. She used a button to push the head of the bed up until she was sitting all the way up. "Isn't it the middle of the school day?"

"Yeah." Tom looked at his feet. "I kind of wanted to see you when no one else was here."

"Why?" asked Jenna.

She didn't sound mad. In fact, it seemed like she was glad to see him. That gave Tom the nerve to say what he had planned.

"I don't think your friends like me very much," Tom said. "And... I wanted to tell you I'm sorry."

"What are you sorry for?" Jenna asked.

Tom took a deep breath. He hoped telling half the truth would be enough. "I'm sorry that we're not friends anymore. I was pretty mean to you last year when we talked."

In his mind, Tom also apologized for the accident.

Jenna smiled. "You know, I've had a lot of time to think this week. In fact, that's about all I've been able to do. One of the things I've thought about is what's really important in life. Two weeks ago, I thought I knew what it was: getting good grades to make my parents happy, being cool to keep my friends happy. But you know what? I never thought about what made *me* happy," Jenna said.

"What does make you happy?" Tom asked.

"I don't know," Jenna replied. "How sad is that?"

Tom shook his head. He didn't know what to say.

"I'm the one who should be sorry, Tom."

"What for?" Tom asked.

"I'm the one who said we were too different to be friends," Jenna said. "But I only said that because I knew my friends were snobs. I was afraid they wouldn't like you. That wasn't fair to you. We used to be really good friends. I was wrong to turn my back on you like that."

"It's okay," Tom said. "We are pretty different."

"Not really," Jenna said. "I hang out with my friends because we're always around each other and we're in all the same classes. But you and I were friends because we were really alike. We enjoyed the same things. We had fun together. That's what's really important. That's what friends should have in common. The rest doesn't really matter."

"Are you saying you want to be friends again?" Tom asked.

"If you want to," Jenna said.

Tom smiled. "I'd like that. I'm really sorry about what happened to you."

"Don't be," Jenna said. "It wasn't your fault."

Tom felt really bad when she said that. He wanted to tell her it was. He even might have, but she kept talking.

"It wasn't anyone's fault, really. A hundred things could have been different and it wouldn't have happened. I could have walked slower or faster that day. Then I wouldn't have been in that place at that moment. Mr. Applewood could have stopped for gas or left the house earlier."

"What about the person in the other car? Don't you blame him?" Tom asked.

"Not really," Jenna said. "Who knows why he ran the red light? Maybe he doesn't even know what happened. I kind of hope he doesn't."

"Really?" Tom was surprised.

"Yeah," Jenna said. "It was an accident. There's no reason for anyone to feel bad. If you think about it, this kind of thing could happen to anyone at any time. One minute, everything's fine. And then, just like that, it's not. Life is too short to worry about what might happen or be angry about what did happen. What's really important is what we do right now. I'm really glad we're friends again, Tom."

"Me too, Jenna. Me too."

Just Like That

11

The next day, Tom took Meera out to dinner for their date. He wanted to take her bowling, but his dad said he was too busy to drive them. He said Tom could take the car if he was careful. There was no way Tom was going to drive again until he got his license.

Tom and Meera walked together to the restaurant. It was starting to get cold.

"I'm sorry my dad couldn't drive us," Tom said.

"Why didn't you just steal a car?" She winked so Tom knew she was joking.

They sat on the same side of the booth. Meera's knee rubbed against Tom's. He liked the way it felt. After the waitress took their order, he held her hand. He was thinking about kissing her when her phone buzzed.

Meera let go of his hand to read her text. She laughed, but didn't tell him what it said. She typed something out and put her phone away. But it buzzed again right away. Tom tried to be patient. Their food came out and he and Meera hadn't talked at all.

He couldn't help but think about Jenna. She wasn't his girlfriend. They were barely even friends again. Yet Jenna took the time to really talk to him. Even when she was in a hospital bed.

Meera was pretty, and a great kisser. Tom wanted more, though.

When they were done eating, Tom walked Meera home.

"Do you want to come in for a while?"

Part of Tom did, but another part didn't.

"Do you like me, Meera?" he asked.

"Of course I do. We're going out, aren't we?"

"I don't know," Tom said. "Are we? You're on your phone more than you talk to me. All we really do together is kiss."

"Don't you like kissing me?" Meera pouted.

Tom knew Evan would tell him to shut up and kiss the girl. A couple of weeks ago, he would have been happy to do that. But he couldn't stop thinking about Jenna. What would it be like to have a girl he could kiss *and* talk to? The thought of kissing Jenna made Tom know what he had to do.

"I do like kissing you. But if that's all we have it's not enough," Tom said.

Meera looked like she might cry for a minute. Then she looked mad.

"I hate you, Tom. You're mean!" she yelled.

She slammed the door and Tom walked away. He thought he might have made a big mistake. He didn't want Meera to be mad at him. She didn't seem to know he had been driving the car that caused Jenna's accident. If she figured it out, it could be bad news for him now.

But he really didn't care. Jenna said life could change just like that. If things had happened a little differently, it could have been him who got hit by Mr. Applewood's car. He didn't want to waste his time with a girl who didn't even want to talk to him.

When he got home, his mom was getting ready for work.

"You got a phone call," she told him. She handed him a piece of paper.

"I need a cell phone."

Tom knew they couldn't afford one. That didn't stop him from asking all the time.

"Me too," his mom laughed.

She was the kind of person who enjoyed life. Tom thought she and Jenna would make good friends.

The message was from Jenna. She was getting out of the hospital tomorrow. She wanted Tom to come to her welcome home party.

"You look happy, Tom." His mom gave him a hug. "I don't think I've seen you smile like that in a long time."

She was right. Tom knew he had done the right thing breaking up with Meera. Getting this message from Jenna was proof.

He hardly slept that whole night. He was very excited to see Jenna. He knew they were only friends, but he hoped they could be more. She must like him, too, if she wanted him to come to her party.

Just Like That

12

Tom's mom drove him to Jenna's house. He wore his best slacks and button-up shirt. When they got to her house, he was nervous.

"I'll pick you up at four o' clock," his mom said. She looked at him and added, "or you can call if you want me to come sooner."

"Thanks, Mom."

He wondered how she always knew how he felt. It made him feel better. He got out of the car and knocked on the door.

Jenna's dad answered. Tom hadn't seen him in five years. He looked a lot older. Tom probably did, too. He didn't think her dad would know who he was.

"Tom! I'm glad you could make it," Jenna's dad said. He shook Tom's hand and led him into the living room.

Jenna sat next to her mom on the couch while the other guests mingled in the room. Jenna wore a yellow dress that matched the yellow cast on her leg. Tom remembered yellow was her favorite color. She said it was the color of happiness.

She smiled when she saw him. "I'm really happy you're here."

"Me too. Thank you for inviting me," Tom said.

"There are snacks in the kitchen if you want some," Mrs. Thompson said.

When Tom got to the kitchen, he saw Sandy. She didn't look happy to see him.

"What are you doing here? Sandy asked.

"Jenna invited me. We're friends," Tom said.

Sandy made a nasty face. "I guess she is brain damaged, after all. I don't know why she would want to be friends with someone like you."

"Sandy!"

Tom and Sandy both jumped. They didn't know Jenna was standing around the corner.

Sandy blushed and looked at her shoes. Tom felt sad for Jenna and mad at Sandy. He wasn't mad because she didn't want him there. He was mad because she was supposed to be Jenna's friend and had said such a mean thing.

Jenna turned around to leave. She almost fell down when her crutch hit the wall. Tom reached out to keep her on her feet.

"Thank you."

"I'm sorry, Jenna," Sandy said. She looked like she was going to cry. "I didn't know you were there."

"So you're not sorry about what you said? Only that I heard? Maybe you should leave, Sandy."

Tom helped Jenna back to the living room. They sat next to each other on the couch. Everyone else stood around talking and eating.

"You know what?" Jenna asked.

"What?"

"I think getting hit by that car was the best thing that ever happened to me," Jenna said. "Now I know who my real friends are."

Tom didn't know what to say. Before he could think of anything, there was a knock at the door. Mr. Thompson answered it. Tom recognized the people from the news. It was Mr. and Mrs. Applewood.

Mr. Applewood moved slowly, but he looked pretty good for a guy who just had a heart attack. Jenna's parents hugged them both. Then they came to sit by Tom and Jenna.

"How are you feeling, dear?" Mrs. Applewood asked Jenna.

"Pretty good. This is my friend, Tom."

Tom shook hands with them both. Mrs. Applewood looked at him for a long time. It seemed like she recognized him. Tom worried she had seen him in the car. But if she had, she would have told the police, right?

They talked for a while. Mrs. Applewood kept giving him funny looks. The longer they were there, the more uncomfortable Tom got. Finally, he had to say something.

"You were in the car when it happened?" he asked Mrs. Applewood.

"I was."

"Did you see the other car?" Tom asked.

She frowned at him. "Not very well. But I'm sure I would know it again if I saw it."

Tom felt like he might throw up. He was sure she knew. "I hope the police find it," he said.

He was so tired of lying, he almost hoped they did.

13

Later that week, Evan drove Tom home from school. He had missed the bus so many times that Evan had started waiting for him, just in case. On this day, Tom had to stay late to finish homework. He had missed too many assignments because he was so worried about the accident all the time.

"I can't believe Mr. Johnson made you stay late," Evan said.

"I'm just glad he didn't give me a detention."

"Want to go to the mall, or something?" Evan asked. "My mom doesn't care if I go out as long as I'm home by dinner."

"Probably not," Tom said. "I should get the rest of my homework done. If I don't, I'll get a detention for sure."

Evan looked a little mad. He wasn't a great student either, but he was better at turning in his work on time. His mom helped him with it after dinner every night. Tom only had his little brother for help.

"Maybe we could study together," Tom said. "Then we'll get done quicker and have more time for video games."

"Maybe."

Tom could tell Evan didn't want to. He knew Evan thought he was smarter than Tom. And he probably was. But he didn't have to be mean about it.

They turned onto their street and saw flashing lights. The police were in front of Mr. Smith's house. They were looking at his car!

Tom almost screamed.

"Whoa. Check it out," Evan said.

Evan didn't seem to understand why the police were there. Evan parked at his house and they walked together back to Tom's house.

Two police officers knocked on Mr. Smith's door. He worked at night like Tom's mom and was probably still asleep. When he answered the door, he was in pajamas.

Tom and Evan stood in the driveway, trying to hear what they said.

"Is this your car, Mr. Smith?"

"Yes, it is," Mr. Smith yawned.

"We've been looking all over this area for a car that looks like this one. We thought the car involved in the accident a couple of weeks ago might belong to someone nearby."

"I don't know anything about that. I heard about it on the news, but that's all."

"Where were you on October fifth at three-thirty in the afternoon?"

Mr. Smith started to look scared. "I was at home, asleep. I work nights and sleep until dinner time."

The police officer wrote something in his notepad.

"Were you alone?"

"Yes. My wife gets home about five-thirty." Mr. Smith frowned. "Do you think I ran that red light? I can tell you, I was asleep. My wife woke me up when she got home."

"We're just checking everything out. Your car does look a lot like the one the girl said she saw. Does anyone else drive it?"

Tom could swear Mr. Smith looked at him. He wondered if Mr. Smith knew.

"I leave the keys in the glove box," he said. "Some of the neighbors ask to borrow my car during the day. I don't want them to wake me up, so I told them to just leave a note if they use it."

"Did anyone borrow your car that day?" The police officer looked very excited, and Tom felt like he might pass out.

"No."

Mr. Smith seemed to look over at Tom again. Tom hoped he was imagining it.

"Is there any chance someone took your car without you knowing?" the police officer asked.

"Maybe."

"Thank you for your time, Mr. Smith. We might have more questions for you later."

Tom took a deep breath of air. He didn't know he had been holding his breath. All he wanted to do was run away. He still thought maybe he should tell the truth about what happened. He didn't want the police to figure it out first.

"Hey, you two." The police officer who had talked to Mr. Smith waved at Tom and Evan.

Evan walked forward to speak to him. Tom stayed back. He was sure the officer would be able to see his guilt in his eyes.

"Do you live around here?" the police officer asked.

"Yes, sir. Down the street. Tom lives right next door, here," Evan said.

"Did either of you see anyone take this car a couple of weeks ago? It would have been on a Tuesday afternoon."

"No, sir." Evan was always super polite around adults. "Tom and I always go to my house after school. We were playing video games that day."

The officer looked from Evan to Tom. "Do you know anyone who might have used this car that day?" he asked.

Tom shook his head. He was afraid to speak.

"All right. If you think of anything, give us a call," the police officer said, before he and the other officer finally drove away.

14

"I guess I'd better start my homework," Tom said. He wanted to get away before Evan could ask him any questions.

Evan followed him into the house.

"Can you believe the police think it was Mr. Smith who hit that girl?" Evan said.

"He didn't hit her," Tom said. "I mean, whoever it was. He only ran a red light. The other car swerved and hit Jenna."

"Whatever," said Evan. "Details."

"There's a huge difference between hitting someone and running a red light," Tom said.

Tom knew he had said too much. Evan looked at him in surprise.

"Wait a minute," Evan said. "That was the day you took Meera out for a ride, wasn't it?"

Tom knew Evan had figured it out. He knew he should be sad or angry or scared. But what he really felt was glad. Now someone else knew. Evan could help him figure out what to do.

"That is so awesome!" Evan said.

This was not what Tom expected Evan to say.

"You told me a car almost hit you," Evan said. "I can't believe I didn't figure it out. Does Meera know?"

"She was too busy looking at her phone," Tom said. "I don't think she even knows I ran a red light."

"Wow. You totally got away with it, Tom. No one has any idea."

"You don't think I should tell someone?" Tom asked. He couldn't believe Evan thought it was cool.

"No way," Evan said. "It's not like you hurt anyone. There's no reason for you to get in trouble."

"You really think so?"

"Sure," Evan said. "If I did something like that, I wouldn't tell anyone. Don't worry. I'll keep your secret."

Tom knew he could count on Evan. The problem was, he didn't know if that was what he wanted anymore.

Just Like That

15

Jenna came back to school a week later.

Tom was very happy to see her. They had talked on the phone many times after the party. He wasn't sure if she would still want to be his friend now that she was back in school.

Since they didn't have any classes together, Tom didn't get to talk to Jenna until lunch. When he got to the cafeteria, he saw Jenna sitting with Sandy. He was glad they had made up and were still friends. But he was sad at the same time. It looked like things would be back to the way they used to be now. He took his sack lunch to a table and sat down to eat.

He usually sat with friends, but today he wanted to be alone.

His sandwich was the same as always, but today it tasted like cardboard.

Tom knew it was because he missed Jenna.

"Mind if I join you?"

Tom looked up to see Jenna standing by his table. He could tell it was hard for her to hold her lunch tray with the crutches. He stood up and took the tray for her. She smiled at him.

"Why are you all by yourself?" she asked.

Tom looked over to the table where Jenna had been sitting. All of her friends were staring at them. Then he looked at his friends. They were staring, too.

"I didn't feel like sitting with my friends today, I guess," Tom said.

"That makes two of us," Jenna said. She sat down and offered Tom some of her fries.

"Everyone is staring at us," he told her.

"Who cares?"

"I do," Tom said.

As soon as he said it, Tom wondered why he cared.

Jenna laughed. "I used to care, too."

"Now you don't?"

"If I've learned one thing lately, it's that life is short," Jenna said. "Even if you live a long time, it's not long enough. Look at Mr. Applewood. He's almost seventy years old. But he said when he had his heart attack it made him think about all the things he still wants to do. I think he's very brave."

"I think you're very brave," Tom said.

Jenna blushed. She looked pretty when she blushed. "I don't think I am. At least, I didn't used to be. But when you almost die, you start to think about what's really important. I used to be afraid all the time. I worried about getting good grades. I worried if my friends would get mad at me about something. I worried about if I would do good in band. I worried about all kinds of stuff."

"I worry about stuff a lot, too," Tom admitted. "How do you stop worrying?"

"You don't," Jenna said. "But you think about what's most important. I still want to get good grades. If I don't, I won't be able to go to a good college. But so what if my friends are mad at me? By tomorrow, they won't be anymore. And if they are, then maybe they weren't such good friends after all."

Jenna looked over at her friends, who had already gone back to their lunches. Tom's friends had also stopped looking at them.

"You're a good friend, Tom. You're a good person."

Tom felt like he was being torn in half.

"Would you still want to be my friend if I wasn't a good person?" Tom asked.

Jenna looked at him. "What do you mean?"

"What if I did something bad?"

Jenna took a long time chewing on her pizza crust. Finally, she took a drink of milk and answered him. "We all do bad things sometimes," Jenna said.

"Yeah. But some things are worse than others." Tom felt very close to crying.

"That's true," Jenna said. "And some things are better than others. We all do good things and bad things all the time. Who we are is more than the things we've done. A really mean person can do lots of good things. That doesn't make her nice. And a really nice person might do something really bad. But he's still a good person."

Tom felt better than he had in a very long time. He felt like Jenna knew him better than anyone else. And she liked him.

They finished eating and Tom took Jenna's tray to the garbage can for her. When he got back, it was almost time to go.

"You know what's most important, Tom?"

"What?" he asked.

"When we do something bad or make a mistake — that's when we have a choice," Jenna said. "When we do the right thing, it's easy. But when we do the wrong thing, we get to choose. That's when you know what kind of person someone really is. I felt really bad when I told you we were too different last year. I knew I should have apologized. But I was too afraid. I feel like I have a second chance now. I want to choose the right thing."

"Me too," Tom said.

He knew deep in his heart what the right thing to do was. He had been too afraid to do it. Jenna thought he was a good person. Now he had to start acting like one.

16

One Year Later...

Tom woke up smiling. Today was the last day of his community service. After today, his Saturdays would be free again. Of course, now he had to get a job.

Tom knew he had gotten off easy. After he told the police he had been driving the car, he could have gone to jail. Instead, he had to do community service and pay a fine. His parents had loaned him the money, but he had to pay them back.

Also, he couldn't get a driver's license until he was eighteen, now. That part, he didn't mind so much. The hardest thing had been the apologies. The judge said he had to say he was sorry to Jenna and Mr. and Mrs. Applewood.

He had gone to the old couple first. He told them the whole story. He told them about Meera and using Mr. Smith's car. He told them about dodging. He told them running the red light had been an accident. He told them how sorry he was.

And then he cried like a baby.

Mr. Applewood wasn't mad. He said he had been young once and had made plenty of mistakes. "I just hope you've learned from this one," he told Tom.

"Yes, sir."

Tom had learned to be polite in front of grownups. He had talked to a lot of police and lawyers and a judge.

Mrs. Applewood didn't want to forgive Tom. "Do you have any idea how much you hurt us?" she asked.

"Yes, ma'am. And I know it could have been a lot worse. If I could do it all over again, I wouldn't get in that car in the first place."

Mrs. Applewood still looked mad. Tom thought it was odd she was more upset than her husband. After talking a long time, she let Tom go.

Telling Jenna was even harder. Her parents were there, too. They did all the talking. Jenna hadn't said a word to him since she found out.

"I just can't believe you didn't tell us," Mrs. Thompson said.

"I'm very sorry," Tom said. "I was scared. At first, I didn't even know it was me. Then when I found out, I didn't know what to do. The longer I waited, the harder it got."

"That's the way it goes with secrets," Mrs. Thompson said. "You think they're helping you, but really they're hurting you. And they hurt everyone else, too."

Tom knew Mrs. Thompson was right. He had hurt a lot of people. His mom was sad. His dad was mad. Joey was scared. Evan thought he was crazy.

Tom knew he deserved it all. So he was very surprised when Jenna called him a few months later.

"I feel like this is the talk in the hall all over again," she said.

"What do you mean?" Tom asked.

"You tried to talk to me, and I wouldn't listen," Jenna said. "This time you told the truth, but I never asked how you felt."

"You don't have to be sorry, Jenna. This was all my fault."

"Do you remember what I told you about making mistakes?" Jenna asked.

"Yes," Tom said. "That's why I decided to tell the truth."

"Well, I made a mistake too," Jenna said. "You did the right thing. The right thing for me to do is to stop being mad at you. I know you're really sorry. And you were really brave to tell the truth. That's the kind of person I want to have as my friend."

* * *

Tom and Jenna started talking on the phone.

Then sitting together at lunch.

Then going out on dates.

Now, they are boyfriend and girlfriend.

Just like that.

About The Author

Jannette LaRoche is a librarian in the Quad Cities, Illinois. She has been working with teenagers for over 15 years, and is passionate about getting the right book into the hands of the right reader at the right time. She is especially interested in connecting teens who don't consider themselves readers with stories that will help them fall in love with books again.

Just Like That

About The Publisher

Story Shares is a nonprofit focused on supporting the millions of teens and adults who struggle with reading by creating a new shelf in the library specifically for them. The ever-growing collection features content that is compelling and culturally relevant for teens and adults, yet still readable at a range of lower reading levels.

Story Shares generates content by engaging deeply with writers, bringing together a community to create this new kind of book. With more intriguing and approachable stories to choose from, the teens and adults who have fallen behind are improving their skills and beginning to discover the joy of reading. For more information, visit storyshares.org.

Easy to Read. Hard to Put Down.